Fairies of Blossom Bakery

Cupcake

and the

Princess Party

Picture Corgi

Acorn
Post Office

Button's House

N

W   E

S

Cookie's House

Bubbles
Hair Salon

Elf
Market

Market

Post
Box

Snail
Nail Bar

A sweet surprise for Sadie Anna Clements — M.A.
To Rosie with love — K.H-J.

FAIRIES OF BLOSSOM BAKERY: CUPCAKE AND THE PRINCESS PARTY A PICTURE CORGI BOOK 978 0 552 56848 7 Published in Great Britain by Picture Corgi, an imprint of Random House Children's Publishers UK A Random House Group Company This edition published 2013

1 3 5 7 9 10 8 6 4 2

Copyright © Random House Children's Publishers UK, 2013 Written by Mandy Archer Illustrated by Kirsteen Harris-Jones The right of Mandy Archer and Kirsteen Harris-Jones to be identified as the author and illustrator of this work has been asserted in accordance with the Copyright, Designs and Patents Act 1988. All rights reserved. Picture Corgi Books are published by Random House Children's Publishers UK, 61–63 Uxbridge Road, London W5 5SA www.randomhousechildrens.co.uk www.randomhouse.co.uk Addresses for companies within The Random House Group Limited can be found at: www.randomhouse.co.uk/offices.htm THE RANDOM HOUSE GROUP Limited Reg. No. 954009 A CIP catalogue record for this book is available from the British Library. Printed in Italy

Fairies of Blossom Bakery

Plum

Cookie

O ver the hills in a land of sweetness,
little fairies bake and play.
Would you like to peep at their secret,
scrumptious world?

Make a wish, then step
into the magic of Fairycake Kingdom
and meet the fairies…

Cupcake

Butterfly

Sparkle

Button

Grand O

Grand
Opening!

Blossom
Bakery

ning!

Rat-a-tat-tat!

Cupcake the fairy peeped round the door of her bakery.

"First batch of the day!" chimed a singsong voice.

It was Cupcake's best friend Cookie, holding a tray full of homemade biscuits. Mmmm . . . the smell was delicious!

Cupcake's tummy fluttered with excitement. Her big dream was about to come true. Today she was to open the Blossom Bakery and Café for the very first time!

All that morning Cupcake's best fairy friends were busy mixing, sifting and sprinkling in the bakery kitchen.

"Hi, Cookie," smiled Button, lifting a tin of triple chocolate brownies out of the oven.

Fairy dust shimmered in the air as Sparkle stirred a bowlful of muffin mixture.

"Time for a little fairy sweetness," beamed Plum, tipping in a bag of plump raisins.

With a touch of her wand, ting! Butterfly filled the kitchen with twinkling fairy lights.

"Everything has to be perfect for the grand opening!" she giggled.

"One, two, three . . ." counted the fairies. "Opening time!"

Cupcake straightened her pinny, then threw back the candy-pink shutters.
"Welcome to Blossom Bakery and Café!" she exclaimed.

Cupcake gasped. A long line of fairies and elves were already standing outside the bakery, clutching golden pennies!

BAKERY
RULES

Wash Hands
Clean Stuff
Be Polite

Grand
Opening!

Soon Cupcake and her friends were rushed off their fairy feet.

"Two chocolate éclairs for table three," said Plum, pulling a tiny notebook out of her apron pocket. "Or was that three éclairs for table two? Oh dear, I'm in a bit of a muddle!"

Grand
Opening!
Blossom
Bakery

Open

Blossom
Bakery

Poor Plum. It seemed as if everybody in Fairycake Kingdom had popped in to try the bakery's delicious treats.

"I'll help you," smiled Cupcake.

All day long the guests poured in. The Grand Opening had been a glittering success. A minute before closing time, the last customer stepped into the bakery.

"Oh my," said Butterfly. "It's the Princess's footman!"
All the fairies curtseyed at once.

"Royal decree for Cupcake," announced the footman,
"from Princess Crystal herself . . ."

Her Royal Highness Crystal
royally appoints

The Blossom Bakery

to deliver a
magical cake
to mark the occasion of her

*Sparkling Springtime Garden Party**

**Please make it sparkly, sweet and
bursting with surprises! C xx*

The footman closed his scroll.

"The party is on Sunday," he said. "Please deliver the cake by sunrise."

"Baking for the Princess?" exclaimed Cupcake. "It will be an honour!"

Cupcake shut the bakery and invited the fairies up to her house for milk and cookies.

"What sort of cake is sparkly, sweet and surprising?" wondered Plum.

"There are heaps of recipe books in your library," said Cookie. "I'll get some . . ."

Cupcake shook her head. "This is something I want to do on my own," she said.

Every evening after the bakery had closed, Cupcake got to work on the royal cake. She baked, whipped and iced every recipe she could think of.

Her mixtures were sweet, her frosting was sparkly, but the fairy couldn't find a surprise that would make a cake fit for a princess.

Tuesday, Wednesday, Thursday came and went. Cupcake still didn't have a plan for the Princess's cake.

"Fairy Academy finished early today," said Plum. "Can I help?"

Cupcake shook her head sadly and closed the door.

On Friday, the friends spotted Cupcake at the Elf Market.

"Look at her," said Sparkle. "She doesn't even want to talk to us."

"Can't stop," called Cupcake. "Too busy."

"Let's go to the Snail Nail Bar if she's going to be like that," sniffed Butterfly.

"Why doesn't she want our help?" asked Button.

It was Saturday evening, and the fairies were in Plum's garden for
a banana-bread supper.

"Where's Cupcake?" asked Cookie.

"Still making the royal cake," guessed Plum.

"We need to go and help her," said Button.

But Cupcake wasn't making the royal cake. She was sitting on a stool in the bakery kitchen, feeling very lonely and very sad.

"None of my recipes is special enough for Princess Crystal!" she sobbed, bursting into tears. "What am I going to do?"

As if by magic, her five fairy friends appeared.

"It's late," said Butterfly, "and we know you're very busy."

"We just wanted to see how you were," added Cookie.

"Please don't go," said Cupcake. "I'm sorry I didn't let you help."

She explained that she wasn't in a rush any more. There would be no grand cake for the Sparkling Springtime Garden Party.

The fairies listened carefully. Then, one by one, they popped their pinnies on.

"This is what friends are for," said Sparkle.

"A truly special cake needs a little extra magic," beamed Cupcake.
"Love, care and sweet fairy wishes!"
  "Six hearts are definitely better than one," added Cookie,
giving her best friend a hug.

Cupcake began to smile.

There wasn't a minute to spare.
  Button fluttered home to fetch more
ingredients, while Sparkle and Cupcake
whipped up the butter and flour.

Cookie warmed up the oven,
then Butterfly made a batch of
her best fairy frosting.

"Now for something truly
surprising," smiled Plum.

The sun was just peeping over Glimmer Mountain when the fairies arrived at the palace.

"Delivery from the Blossom Bakery," called Cupcake.

Princess Crystal glided into the ballroom and stepped forward to unveil not one baked creation, but a sparkly, spellbinding tower of mini cupcakes.

"Enchanting!" gasped Her Royal Highness.

"They're not just my work," said Cupcake proudly. "My friends all helped."

"Then you shall all come to the party," replied the Princess, "as my royal guests."

Cupcake beamed. Her bakery was a success, the Princess had her cake, and it was all thanks to the magic of true fairy friends.

Princess Party pink fairy cupcakes

Cupcakes with pink buttercream icing, sprinkled with sweet toppings

Shopping list for 12 cupcakes and buttercream icing

Cupcakes
- 110g self-raising flour
- 110g caster sugar
- 110g margarine
- 1 teaspoon baking powder
- 1½ teaspoons vanilla extract
- 2 eggs
- Paper cupcake cases

Buttercream Icing
- 150g soft butter
- 275g icing sugar
- 2 tablespoons milk
- A few drops of pink food colouring

- Edible sugar stars to decorate

To make the cupcakes:

1. Ask a grown-up to pre-heat the oven to 160°C/325°F/Gas Mark 3. Put 12 paper cupcake cases into the holes in a muffin tray.

2. Put the flour, sugar, margarine and baking powder into a large mixing bowl with a teaspoon of vanilla extract. Crack the eggs into the bowl and mix the ingredients together. Use a wooden spoon or ask for help to combine everything with an electric mixer until the mixture feels fluffy and light.

3. Spoon the mixture into the cupcake cases and ask your grown-up to put the muffin tray into the oven. The cupcakes need about 20 minutes to rise and cook through – they will be golden brown when done. Ask your adult to take them out of the oven and place them on a wire rack to cool down.

Always ask a grown-up to help you in the kitchen, especially when using the oven.

To make the delicious buttercream icing:

4. Put all the ingredients for the buttercream icing into a bowl.

5. Mix everything up until the icing looks creamy and good enough to eat. If it is still too thick, add a little more milk, a few drops at a time.

Now it's time to ice the cupcakes!

6. When the cupcakes have cooled down, spoon a bit of the icing on the top of the cupcake, then fluff it up with a fork.

7. Take a pinch of sugar stars and sprinkle them over the cupcakes. Princess perfect!

Fairy Tip
Fairies always wash their hands before starting a new recipe!

Bye-bye for now!

We hope you enjoyed your visit
to the Fairycake Kingdom.

Please join us again for more adventures!